Training Horses is a v

reminded me of the ancient Christian wisdom which understood that many of our spiritual shortcomings in fact stem from our virtues. Too often misunderstood aspects of a child's personality result in disruptive and ineffective behavior that can become a source of parental frustration, power-struggles, and shame in our children. This cycle of frustration only serves to reinforce problem behavior, low self-esteem in our children, and erode the parent-child bond. This book takes an approach that can help parents break free from this trap. This is an imaginative, fun, and strength-based way to help children accept all of themselves and take responsibility for their own character development; something every committed parent wants. I suspect that parents might learn a thing or two about the transforming power of God's love and acceptance on the way.

David Pillar, M.Div
Pastoral Counselor
Licensed Marriage and Family Therapist

The principles in *Trading Horses* were excellent and had several underlying principles that will pay great blessings for parents in the journey of raising children. Most parents may think that the journey is over when your children are off on their own and involved in a career. Nothing is farther from the truth. We are still training horses even though our children are 28, 26, and 24. We also have two grandchildren that can be added to the journey of raising children. As long as the parents, children, and grandchildren are alive, these principles can be used to help one another grow in the grace and knowledge of our Lord and Savior Jesus Christ.

Mike Cagle

GracePointe Community Church

Marietta, GA

TRAINING HORSES

Guiding Your Child Toward a First Place Finish

TRAINING HORSES

Deahdra-Lynn Atencio

TATE PUBLISHING & *Enterprises*

Published by Tate Publishing & Enterprises, LLC
127 E. Trade Center Terrace | Mustang, Oklahoma 73064 USA
1.888.361.9473 | www.tatepublishing.com

Tate Publishing is committed to excellence in the publishing industry. The company reflects the philosophy established by the founders, based on Psalm 68:11,
"The Lord gave the word and great was the company of those who published it."

Book design copyright © 2008 by Tate Publishing, LLC. All rights reserved.
Cover design and Interior design by Jennifer L. Fisher
Illustration by Jason Hutoon

Published in the United States of America

ISBN: 978-1-60604-044-7
1. Christian Living: Relationships   2. Youth & Children: Children: Activities
08.05.20

Dedicated to my mom for inspiring me to find what works and for not throwing out her first waffle, my children for being my waffles, and most importantly my husband, my love, and my best friend. Without you, my inspiration would have no waffles.

Thanks to Verb1 Productions,

www.verb1.net

for the author photo.

Training Horses

Have you ever seen a baby horse? A baby horse is called a colt. I grew up on a horse farm, so I saw lots of colts. One day, Daddy gave my sister and me two colts to train as our own. We nearly jumped out of our riding boots as Daddy led the two colts from the barn to the training field. We expected to ride them that very minute, but the colts jumped and ran around, not listening to us at all.

"Horses aren't born trained," Daddy explained. "You need to train them to obey your commands."

We had watched Daddy train horses for years, and he made it look so easy. We were sure we would be riding our horses by sunset.

As the sun set that first day, my sister and I flopped on the grass, frustrated and disappointed. Daddy encouraged us by saying, "It will take a lot of work, love, and strength from you both, but a trained horse is something to be very proud of." Daddy sat down between us and put his arms around us. "I don't expect you to do this by yourselves. I will always be here to help you."

At first we worked every day with both horses. The first horse was rather easy to train, and we were riding him in a very short time. Daddy named him Good Morning. Every day we'd wake up early, eat a quick breakfast, and ride Good Morning.

The other horse didn't seem to want to be trained. He would struggle and fight with us about everything. So, we started to give up on him and spend all our time with Good Morning. Daddy named the more difficult horse Today and said the longer we ignored Today the harder he would be to train.

The day came when we could not ignore Today any longer. He was not able to be with the other horses, and he was always kicking the fence. Daddy said that if we didn't train him, we would be responsible for any trouble he caused.

At first, Today wouldn't even come to the side of the fence when we called him. Daddy asked us if we were going to be the master of Today or if he was going to be our master.

"Who's going to be the boss?" Daddy asked.

So we started the long process of training Today. We had to get him to wear the saddle and bit and teach him to obey our commands. Some days seemed easier than others. If we went a few days without working with him, he would forget some of what we'd already taught him.

After a long struggle, Today was trained. We could ride him anytime we wanted. He seemed to look forward to us coming with our saddle. He turned out to be one of our strongest and fastest horses on the farm. We learned quickly that even after being trained, if we didn't ride him for a while, he would seem to forget us and our saddle.

We learned a lot from Good Morning and Today, not only about training horses, but also about training ourselves. After both horses were trained, Daddy told us why he had chosen the names Today and Good Morning.

"See, children, you wake up with smiles on your faces. Your mother and I look forward to seeing your big grins bouncing down the stairs for breakfast. That is why I named the easier horse Good Morning. God makes every new day for us and wants us to rejoice in it. Having a good morning was not hard for you. So, I named the easier horse something that was easy for you."

"Training Today was much harder. He took more work and more time. There were many days where you didn't work with him at all, and he became even harder to train," Daddy explained. "It is important to do what needs to be done when it needs to be done, such as cleaning your room. You tell Mom and me that you will do it tomorrow because you would rather play outside. But by the next day, the mess is bigger and harder to clean up.

Once you get in there and clean your room, you do a good job, but sometimes toys get stepped on and broken before you get them picked up. It's not wrong to play outside; it's good for you, but we also need to choose wisely when we have other responsibilities. I named the more difficult horse Today to remind you to do today what needs to be done today."

That is the day I learned that we all have horses to train. The gifts and talents God has given each of us are sometimes like wild horses. Left untrained, they can be destructive and cause us a lot of trouble. An untrained horse will take its rider places he or she doesn't want to go. A well-trained horse is a beautiful, strong blessing, bringing its rider safely and quickly to his or her destination. We have to choose whether we are going to use our talents and gifts or whether they are going to use us. To ride

a horse and receive the blessings of its strength, we must train it. None of our horses are bad, but some are running wild. God made each of us, and no one is bad, but we all have some behaviors that need to be controlled and trained.

Daddy also told us about his first horse and how Granddad named it Soft Voice.

"Your Grandmamma was always reminding me to use a soft voice indoors. She would tell me my strong, loud voice would be a blessing for God someday, but I also needed to learn how great a soft voice could be. I'm now a great speaker. I enjoy telling people how much God loves them. I can also call you kids from a long way off, but I also learned how to use my soft voice. When someone is afraid or worried, I use my soft voice to give comfort. When someone needs a prayer during the night, I can pray softly without waking up others.

Recognizing that our horses are blessings and not burdens is the first step. God's plan for you is a good one, and He wants to help all of us train the horses he blesses us with."

Since then I've had many horses to train. Each time God gave me a new horse, I learned to train it better. I still get new horses, and some are still hard to train, but with God's help, I get it done.

God blesses all of us, and I'm sure some of your horses have been hard to train. Can you think of any horses you might need to train right now? Maybe your parents can help you. Why don't you color some horses and give them names? Then you can work on training those horses. I hope you have as much fun becoming the master of your horses as I do. I look forward to the blessings God has for both you and me.

Note to parents

There are no hard-and-fast rules for teaching your children how to train their horses. The goal is for your children to care about their behavior and most importantly, to be children who please God. Each of our horses is a gift from God that molds us into the people He wants us to become. Here are some guidelines to get you started. Please make any changes necessary to perfect this for your children and family.

- First, create a "board." One side should represent the untrained and less-appealing side. The other is the green, safe, or trained side. Fasten paper or cardstock horses with magnets, hook-and-loop stickers from a fabric or craft store, or paper clips. We've also enjoyed making the horses out of shrinking paper, which you can also buy at craft stores.

- Instruct your children to choose and color their own horses.

- First instruct the children to color a couple of horses that can already be "rode" to reflect behaviors that the children do not struggle with. Place these horses in the trained area.

- Discuss with your children the honor they will feel when they become the master of their horses.

- Use Bible verses to explain behavior that is and is not pleasing to God.

- Regularly instruct your children to move their own horses from the untrained to the trained area of the board, based on joint evaluation. Do they feel overall that they worked hard (not necessarily that they rode their horses perfectly all the time, but that they made an effort), or were they not trying to "ride their horses"? When reminded to "get back on their horses," did they do it? Guide your children in the evaluation of the day. Help them see when and how they put forth effort and when or how they did not.

- Avoid other incentives or rewards for moving the horses forward. The reward should be their own accomplishment of becoming the "boss" and "riding" their horses. You can, however, point out blessings that come from the changes in their behavior.

- Having a horse doesn't free children to make all the "bad choices" they want and avoid other natural or logical choices. Whenever possible, moving back their horses to the untrained side should be their discipline. If a child, for example, is working on being more careful with his or her body movements in the house, and you notice the child slowing down while playing indoors, don't offer him or her a treat. Instead, invite the child to move his or her horse. If the child is not being careful and breaks something while running through the house, move the child's horse back to the untrained area. At the same time, the broken object may still have to be replaced. That is a logical consequence.

- How often you move a horse is completely

dependent on your child. If a specific behavior recurs every hour, for example, a horse reflecting that behavior may move back and forth all day. A horse reflecting a less-frequent behavior may only move once a day. Look for times that your children are "riding their horses" and let them move their horses forward. Observe the behaviors and their corresponding horses, and note the frequency at which each horse moves.

- Use positive names when naming horses.

  » When choosing horses, look for behavior that you want trained, changed, controlled, or mastered. It is important for both parents and children to see the difference between the motivation and the behavior. While it might be tempting to only see negative behavior, please remember that there are no bad children or bad horses. Using positive names for your horses will help you and your children see the value in their horses.

» Likewise, the motivation behind a specific behavior is neither good nor bad. The horse is the motivation—the action, behavior, or results may be undesirable. The child who yells or screams, for example, could name his or her horse "soft voice," "outdoor voice," "whisper," "public speaker," "crowd voice," or "acting voice." Even though the loud voice is a blessing (motivation), the timing and place are the problems (action or result). As another example, a child who is "nosey," or always asking questions, is a seeker of knowledge (motivation). Encourage him or her to seek knowledge in God, academics, or facts. Seeking knowledge is not bad, but the people involved, as well as the timing, places, and circumstances can be inappropriate for that type of behavior. Show your children pleasing and appropriate times to use their gifts. On one occasion, a boy who was good at seeking knowledge and very academically advanced was at school one day when his teacher instructed the children in the class to stack their chairs and line up at the door. The boy couldn't resist asking "Why? What are we doing? Are we going outside?" Unfortunately, the teacher became annoyed because she perceived this as disobedience, when the boy was only seeking knowledge. But when the boy asks questions during lessons, she's excited and proud of his quest for knowledge. When he acted this way when instructed to stack his chair and line up with the rest of the class, however, she became upset, and the boy became confused.

» Let your children name their own horses. You can guide and encourage appropriate names, but each child's involvement is very important for producing a sense of ownership.

- Choose positive and motivating words:

  » Emphasize pride, joy, accomplishment, and honor in training.

  » Emphasize the children's power, ability,

and strength given to them from God to become the boss, master, ruler, or controller of their behavior.

» Remember that God gave these horses to your children and should not be left out of the equation. Your children should know that God has a plan for their lives, and He will help them meet the goals He has set for them. Pray every day for and with your children. Ask God to help your children use the strength He has provided to make the right choices. Thank God for the blessing of the horses your children are training.

- Look for ways to build the strength and pride of a horse. The child who yells can go to a park, measure how far you can walk, and still hear his or her yells. Try this exercise. Walk across a football field or beach shore until you can't hear the child's voice. Then say, "Wow! I can get that far and still hear you. God has really given you a strong voice. Now, which jobs need a strong voice?" And let the child come up with positive uses for his or her strong voice. Give the child times to use that voice, such as acting or voice classes. Plan regular trips to the park where the child can be loud. Get creative!

- Share excitement when your children move their horses forward. Acknowledge and sympathize with your children's own disappointments and share your feelings, being very careful never to shame the children or cause them to feel guilty.

Just like real horses take different amounts of energy and time to train, so will your childrens' horses. Our first horse was named Going Home.

Every time I arrived to pick our son up from a specific play date, he would stomp, cry, and yell that he didn't want me there. We were glad he was enjoying his friends and understood that he didn't like leaving, but his disrespectful behavior was unacceptable. The day after we named Going Home and placed the horse in the untrained area of the board, our son saw me arrive to pick him up, stomped one foot, smiled a great big grin, and "trotted" over as if he were riding his horse. He was thrilled with the control and power he had over his behavior.

Another horse was not so easy. Right Path really challenged our resolve to this system. We don't expect our children to never stray off the narrow road, but we do want them to return to the right path when given wise direction. One of our children often struggled with making that choice.

Sticking to one's decisions and having strong convictions will be a great blessing as our child grows and leaves the shelter of our home, but the "I'm not changing my mind or behavior" attitude is not appreciated when it strays off that right path. We needed to look our child in the eye and provide clear directions for how to correct the behavior. The horse named Right Path only needed to take good advice and act on it. We would clearly explain exactly what his choices were, and which choice would be riding Right Path. It took a while for our child to make the right choice. We would say, "You are letting Right Path get out of control. Get back on that horse." The response would be a defiant "I don't care!" or "NO!" And there were consequences for making behavior choices that were off the right path. Eventually we could just say with a wink, "Right Path," and the right choice would be made.

Horses are not just for children. Don't be afraid to put your own horses on the board. Admitting to our children that we also struggle makes it much easier for us to "ride our horses." It is a form of accountability that builds their trust and respect for us. There are horses in our lives that our children should not be burdened with. Don't share private, adult problems that would worry the child. Sharing struggles like washing the dishes, folding the laundry, or even driving the speed limit are possibilities. Once I've shared a horse with my children, it is much easier to control it. Be prepared for your children to be supportive and even "call you on it" when you're not riding your horse. My son would move my horse for me. He would notice and even compliment me when he saw me working hard on a horse. It can be a little alarming at first to listen to your children talk about your faults, but I found it very helpful.

Take this idea and really make it your own. Work with your family and find the words and techniques that work best for all of you. Sit down together and talk about this. Read the story often. If possible, visit a horse stable and learn more about horses. And know that this is only one tool used in raising children. I pray that God will guide you in the ways that are best for your family.